Hello, Family Members,

Learning to read is one of the most in of early childhood. **Hello Reader!** bo_____ children become skilled readers who like to read. Beginning readers learn to read by remembering frequently used words like "the," "is," and "and"; by using phonics skills to decode new words; and by interpreting picture and text clues. These books provide both the stories children enjoy and the structure they need to read fluently and independently. Here are suggestions for helping y___ ____ ___ during, _____ ___ ading:

Before
- Look at the cover and pictures and have your child predict what the story is about.
- Read the story to your child.
- Encourage your child to chime in with familiar words and phrases.
- Echo read with your child by reading a line first and having your child read it after you do.

During
- Have your child think about a word he or she does not recognize right away. Provide hints such as "Let's see if we know the sounds" and "Have we read other words like this one?"
- Encourage your child to use phonics skills to sound out new words.
- Provide the word for your child when more assistance is needed so that he or she does not struggle and the experience of reading with you is a positive one.
- Encourage your child to have fun by reading with a lot of expression . . . like an actor!

After
- Have your child keep lists of interesting and favorite words.
- Encourage your child to read the books over and over again. Have him or her read to brothers, sisters, grandparents, and even teddy bears. Repeated readings develop confidence in young readers.
- Talk about the stories. Ask and answer questions. Share ideas about the funniest and most interesting characters and events in the stories.

I do hope that you and your child enjoy this book.

—Francie Alexander
Reading Specialist,
Scholastic's Instructional Publishing Group

If you have questions or comments about how children learn to read, please contact Francie Alexander at FrancieAl@aol.com

To Super-Tutor Rosemary Hall
— K.M.

To Wills and Georgia
— M.S.

Text copyright © 1998 by Kate McMullan.
Illustrations copyright © 1998 by Mavis Smith.
All rights reserved. Published by Scholastic Inc.
HELLO READER! and CARTWHEEL BOOKS and associated logos
are trademarks and/or registered trademarks of Scholastic Inc.

Library of Congress Cataloging-in-Publication Data
McMullan, Kate.
    Fluffy's silly summer/by Kate McMullan; illustrated by Mavis Smith.
        p.   cm. — (Hello reader! Level 3)
    "Cartwheel books."
    Summary: Having gone home with Maxwell for summer vacation, Fluffy the classroom guinea pig goes swimming, enters a contest, and investigates a jungle.
    ISBN 0-590-46287-3
    [1. Guinea pigs — Fiction.]   I. Smith, Mavis, ill.   II. Title.   III. Series.
PZ7.M47879Fs   1998
[E] — dc21   97-45006
                                                                          CIP
                                                                           AC

10   9 8 7 6 5 4 3 2 1   8 9/9 0/0 01 02

Printed in the U.S.A.   24
First printing, April 1998

87057

FLUFFY'S
SILLY SUMMER

by Kate McMullan

Illustrated by Mavis Smith

Hello Reader! — Level 3

SCHOLASTIC INC.
Cartwheel ·B·O·O·K·S·®

New York   Toronto   London   Auckland   Sydney

Fluffy the Hero

Fluffy went home with Maxwell
for summer vacation.
Oh, boy! thought Fluffy.
I will nibble grass.
I will lie in the sun.
I love summer!

Maxwell put Fluffy's cage in the den.

He gave Fluffy seeds and water.

"I'm going to the park,"
Maxwell told Fluffy.

"I will see you later!"

Wait! thought Fluffy. **What will _I_ do?**

Maxwell's sister, Violet,
came into the den.
"Are you tired of being in that cage?"
she asked Fluffy.
You got that right, thought Fluffy.
"Do you want to go outside with me?"
asked Violet.
Do I ever! thought Fluffy.
Take me to the grass!

Violet picked Fluffy up.
"I'm going to take you swimming,"
she said.
Take me WHAT? thought Fluffy.

Hey! Stop! Wait a second!
thought Fluffy. **I am a land animal!**
I walk. I run. I even trot.
But I do NOT swim!

Violet carried Fluffy outside
to her wading pool.
She put him on the back of a yellow duck.
She pushed the duck
toward the middle of the pool.
"Whee!" she said.

The duck bounced up and down.
Fluffy held onto the duck's neck.
Easy, big fellow, he said to the duck.
I don't want to get wet!

Violet jumped into the wading pool.
"Isn't this fun?" she said.
Not yet, thought Fluffy.

Violet kicked and splashed.
"Whee!" she said.
The duck bounced up and down.
Stop! thought Fluffy. **Whoa, Duckie!**

Then Fluffy saw a fin in the water.
A shark was swimming toward Violet!
Fluffy had to save her!

Go! Go! Go! Fluffy called to his duck.
Fluffy rode toward the shark.
Faster! he called to his duck.

The duck carried Fluffy
over to the shark.
Fluffy hit the shark on the head.
He popped it in the nose.
Fluffy hit him again, right in the teeth!
That did it.
The shark rolled over.

Fluffy the Hero rode his duck
over to Violet.

You are safe now, Violet, thought Fluffy.

That shark will not hurt you.

Violet picked Fluffy up.

No, no, do not thank me,

thought Fluffy the Hero.

I was only doing my job.

Violet dunked Fluffy in the water.

"Whee!" she cried.

A hero's life is never easy,
thought Fluffy.

A Prize for Fluffy

Maxwell, Wade, and Emma
read a sign in a pet shop window.
It said:

BEST PETS CONTEST

Is your pet good-looking?
Is your pet smart?
Can your pet do a trick?
Bring your pet to
Mr. Small's Pet Shop
on Saturday at 1:00.
There will be
PRIZES
for the best pets.

"Fluffy could win a prize," Emma said.

A prize? thought Fluffy.

I'll win ALL the prizes!

On Saturday morning,
Emma washed Fluffy's face and ears.
Maxwell washed Fluffy's paws.
Wade turned him over
and washed his tummy.

Enough! thought Fluffy.

I'm not going for the CLEAN prize!

"We want to enter Fluffy
in the contest," Maxwell told Mr. Small.
You are looking at the big winner!
thought Fluffy.
Mr Small wrote down Fluffy's name.

All kinds of pets came for the contest.
But there was only one other guinea pig.
Maxwell put Fluffy down beside it.
I am a crested pig,
the other guinea pig told Fluffy.
She scratched her head. **I am
going to win this contest.**

Fluffy's eyes got very big.

The other guinea pig was Kiss!

Kiss did not seem to remember Fluffy.

But Fluffy remembered her.

Kiss had eaten his valentine apple.

Kiss had said his toys were junk.

Fluffy did not like Kiss.

I am beautiful, Kiss told Fluffy.

I am smart. I can do a million tricks.

I will win all the prizes.

I don't think so, said Fluffy.

"Kiss!" called Mr. Small.

A girl took Kiss onto the stage.

Kiss turned around.

Kiss counted to one.

Kiss rolled over.

Fluffy thought Kiss was very good.

He bit his nails.

Can I beat her? he wondered.

Did you see me? Kiss asked
when her turn was over. **I was
really great, wasn't I?**

Kiss scratched her head again.
Fluffy saw some dark spots on her crest.
Kiss had fleas!
One of her fleas jumped onto Fluffy.
Yikes! thought Fluffy.

"Fluffy!" called Mr. Small.

Maxwell carried Fluffy onto the stage.

He put Fluffy down.

Fluffy shook his head.

He shook his arms and his legs.

He had to get that flea off!

Fluffy skipped across the stage.
"Go, Fluffy!" called Wade.

Fluffy turned upside down
and kicked his feet.
"What a pig!" called Emma.

Fluffy scratched his head with one paw.

He rubbed his tummy with the other.

He had to get rid of that flea!

The flea was on Fluffy's head.

All of Fluffy's jumping around had
made the flea very dizzy.

The flea jumped off Fluffy.

Yes! thought Fluffy.

The flea was gone!

He pumped his paw in the air as he
ran off stage.

"Here is a prize," said Mr. Small.
"It is for the best dancer...Fluffy!"
Everyone clapped and clapped.

"Wow," Maxwell said.
"How did Fluffy
get to be such a good dancer?"
I think I will keep that a secret,
thought Fluffy.

Big, Bad Fluffy

Maxwell took Fluffy out to the backyard.
Fluffy looked around.
It's a jungle out here! he thought.
"Keep an eye on Fluffy, Maxwell,"
said his mom.
"Don't worry," said Maxwell.
"Fluffy won't go anywhere."

Maxwell lay down in the backyard.

He put Fluffy down next to him.

Maxwell watched Fluffy nibble grass.

He watched him sniff the ground.

Maxwell closed his eyes.

Fluffy wandered away.

In the jungle, thought Fluffy,
danger is everywhere.

Fluffy walked into the jungle.

A lion poked his head out of the brush.

Get back! thought Fluffy.

**You do NOT want to mess
with a big, bad pig!**

The lion ran back into the brush.

Fluffy made his way through the jungle.

A snake lay in his path.

Go away! thought Fluffy.

Or I will tie you in a big, bad knot!

The snake crawled off.

Fluffy walked deeper into the jungle.
A tiger jumped out at him.

You don't scare me! thought Fluffy.
I'm big! And I'm bad!
The tiger hurried away.

Fluffy smiled.
It is good to be big and bad,
he thought.

Suddenly a dog barked at Fluffy.

Fluffy jumped! He started running.

He saw a hole at the bottom of a tree.

He dove into it to hide.

But the hole was not empty.

It was full of baby rabbits.

Fluffy saw the dog
running for the rabbit hole.
Fluffy jumped into the nest
of baby rabbits.

The dog stuck its head
into the rabbit hole.
Fluffy tried to look
like a cute little bunny.

The dog went away.
Sometimes, thought Fluffy,
it is good to be little and cute.

Just then, Mama Rabbit came home.
Mama Rabbit picked up
one of her babies.
She picked up another one.
She bent down to pick up Fluffy.
Uh oh, thought Fluffy.

You are not one of my babies!
Mama Rabbit said.
She growled at Fluffy.
**Get out of my nest
or you will be sorry!**

Fluffy leaped out of the nest.
He jumped out of the rabbit hole.
He ran across the backyard
straight to Maxwell.

Maxwell opened his eyes.
"I knew you would not go anywhere,"
he said to Fluffy.
Maxwell picked Fluffy up and took him
inside.

Sometimes, thought Fluffy,
it is good to be home.